Oh No, Rosie!

Written by Pippa Goodhart

Illustrated by Sian James

Collins

Chapter 1

Megan threw herself face down on to her bed and whisper-howled into her pillow. "It's not FAIR!"

Old Mr Toby, downstairs, mustn't hear that she was upset. It wasn't his fault. It wasn't even his dog's fault. Was it Mum's fault? Megan curled up tight. Mum should have understood!

All her life, until five days ago, Megan had lived in the village of Barton. She'd gone to the village playgroup; then the village school. She knew lots of people in the village. Best of all, she'd had Lola as her best friend. Then everything had changed.

It began with Mum spending lots of time
on her phone and frowning in a way that
gave Megan a horrible fluttery feeling of
worry in her tummy.

When Megan came home from school
one day, there was a rich chocolatey cooking
smell when they opened the front door.
Mum had been cooking a treat, but on
a day when they didn't have visitors.

"Why are we having muffins?" said Megan.

"I thought you'd like them," said Mum.
Then she saw Meggie's face. "Sit down, sweetheart.
I've got something to tell you."

"What?"

"It's exciting, really," began Mum.

"What?" said Megan again, more firmly.
The muffins on the plate between them
stayed untouched.

"We're going to move house to Eskton," said Mum.

Megan's stomach felt as if it had dropped to the floor. Thud. So that's what the muffins were for.

"Moving to Eskton?" said Megan. Eskton was a whole long bus ride away from Barton. "Why?"

"I've found us a nice house near to a good school," said Mum.

"What?" Megan stood up. "You mean I've got to go to a different school?!"

She'd protested, of course. She'd told Mum she'd go and live with Lola so she could stay in the village, and Mum could move without her. But when you're a child, you sometimes just have to do what the grown-ups decide. Megan felt sick. Her heart and her mind were racing with thoughts and feelings.

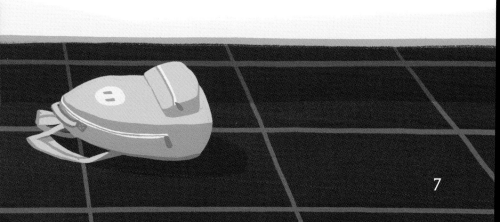

Chapter 2

The new house in town smelt different and sounded different from their old home. This one didn't feel like home.

Mum showed Megan a map and pointed out Barton and Eskton. "See? We haven't moved all that far. We'll visit Lola, and Lola can visit here."

"But I won't see her every day," said Megan. "It isn't the same." She felt lost and scared.

Walking to the new school on her first day, Megan had looked around and tried to remember her way back to her new home. "You've got to fetch me at the end of the day," she said to Mum, grabbing hold of Mum's jacket.

"Of course, I will," Mum had smiled. "Now go in, Meggie. I know it's scary, but I'm sure you'll soon make new friends."

Megan's new teacher was Mr Patel.

"Let's see, which table has a space where Megan can sit?" he'd said. He and Megan had looked around the room, and the children had all looked back. There was no space. "Verity, can you move up and let Megan sit beside you, please?"

"Do I *have* to?" said the girl called Verity. She did move up just a bit. Then she put her arm over her work as if she thought Megan was going to copy. There was another girl sitting at the table too. Megan thought that she and Lola might not have liked it if they were told to share with a new girl.

"Thank you," she muttered, but the girls didn't say anything back.

When it came to playtime, the children rushed outside. Megan followed and then stood by the door, watching. They were all running after footballs or sitting in huddles on the benches, giggling over things that Megan couldn't quite hear.

Is Lola lonely without me? wondered Megan. *I sort of hope that she is.*

13

When Mum came to fetch Megan, Megan told her, "I'm not going to this school again. They don't like me, and I don't like them."

"I'm sure you'll soon make friends, Meggie," said Mum.

As they walked home across the park, everybody else seemed to have a friend already. There were people walking in pairs or groups. Even the people on their own were talking to others on phones. Or they had a dog friend.

If I had a dog, thought Megan, *I'd have a friend. If I get a cute little puppy, then the children at that school will all want to stroke it. They might want to come home with me to play with the puppy, and then become my friends!* She suddenly felt light and bouncy with hope.

"Mum," she said. "I need a dog."

"Oh, good," said Mum.

That surprised Megan! "Really?" Megan did a skip.

"Yes," said Mum. "It's good because I know just the dog we can have. Wait and see!" Mum wouldn't tell her any more than that. Megan rang Lola.

"I'm getting a dog! Well, a puppy, I hope. A really fluffy one. I'm going to –" But Lola interrupted her.

"That's nice," said Lola. "My new friend's got this really fluffy pencil case."

"What new friend?" said Megan, feeling suddenly tight inside.

"She's called Penny," said Lola. "She's not as nice as you, of course, Megs. But she's funny, and she's got this huge bedroom with –" And Lola went on talking, with Megan not listening anymore.

Megan was busy thinking over and over, *Lola's already replaced me!* But at least Megan had the puppy to look forward to. Lola would want to visit and see a puppy. Perhaps that was something Penny didn't have?

Chapter 3

"Somebody special is about to arrive," said Mum, with a big smile.

"Who?"

"Your dog!" laughed Mum.

When the doorbell rang, Megan ran to open the door and there, in front of her, was …

"Mr Toby?" said Megan.

Mr Toby had his middle-aged daughter with him. He had a walking stick in one hand, and a lead in the other. Next to him was his old dog, Rosie. Megan stood there, her mouth open, her mind a scribble of thoughts.

"Come in!" said Mum to the visitors. Then she turned to Megan. "Mr Toby is going to live in a care home where he can be looked after. He'll have a nice room of his own. But dogs aren't allowed there. So old Rosie needs a new home, and I've told Mr Toby that you want a dog. So that's perfect, isn't it? Surprise!"

It certainly was a surprise. Megan stared at plump brown Rosie slumped on the floor. Megan could smell her old dog sort of smell.

"We'll give Rosie a good home, won't we?" said Mum to Megan.

"Oh, I do hope so," said Mr Toby. "I couldn't bear for her to go to people she didn't know."

Megan looked at Mr Toby's pleading and hopeful eyes, and she made her mouth smile upwards for him.

Then she bent down to pat Rosie, hoping that Mr Toby hadn't guessed her real feelings. *Yap!* went Rosie. *Yap, yap!* Megan snatched her hand away. *She doesn't like me,* thought Megan. And *I don't like her.*

"I've got to do my reading homework," Megan had said, before running upstairs and throwing herself on to her bed.

Not fair!

Megan thought of the sweet puppy she'd hoped for. She thought of the yappy old dog downstairs, and she cried. She thought of Lola with Penny, and she cried some more. Then she thought of how Rosie had had to leave her best friend, Mr Toby, and she felt a bit sorry for the dog. *Am I being mean?* She and Rosie had both had to leave their home and their best person. Perhaps they did sort of belong together?

Megan sat up. She wiped the tears off her face with the back of a hand, took a deep breath and went back downstairs.

Chapter 4

Mr Toby and his daughter had gone. Rosie was by the front door, whimpering because she'd been left behind.

"Poor old Rosie," said Mum.

"Shall we give her a walk?" said Megan.

"That's a good idea," said Mum. "A quick walk in the park."

Megan felt a bit wary, reaching down to snap the
lead on to Rosie's collar. "Good girl, Rosie," she said.
Rosie didn't yap. Megan patted Rosie's hard rough coat
that was so different from soft puppy fur, and sighed.

Rosie was glad to get outside,
wagging her stubby little tail.

Megan set off along the path into
the park as Mum lagged behind,
busy on her phone. There were children
on the swings up ahead.

"Let's run," said Megan, thinking she'd
run past the children so that she didn't
have to talk to them. But Rosie was slow,
dragging on the lead. Then Rosie suddenly
stopped, and Megan had to stop too.
"Oh no, Rosie!" said Megan. "Move!"
But Rosie was sniffing, nose down in
the grass. The children on the swings
turned to look.

"Come ON, Rosie!" said Megan. She gave
up tugging at the lead and tried to push
Rosie instead. She could hear laughter,
as she heaved Rosie behind some shrubs
so that they could hide from the children.

Megan felt hot tears welling. She bent over and hugged Rosie's solid body. It was comforting, stroking that rough coat. "Oh, Rosie," she whispered.

But Rosie was soon bored of being held tight. She pulled away and began to sniff around the grass again. Megan could see Mum, still on her phone, but she didn't want to go to the path past the swings yet. She sat, cross-legged, holding Rosie's lead as the old dog snuffled around. Rosie's stubby tail wagged happily as she found a good smell. That made Megan smile. Then, *snuffle*, Rosie's nose was wetly in Megan's ear, making her laugh.

"Are you bored, Rosie?" said Megan. "Shall we go home?"

Megan stood up and led Rosie towards where
Mum was waiting on a bench. She was feeling
quite cheerful, until she saw Verity and Rubinda
up ahead. They saw Megan at the same moment.
Rubinda and Verity looked at each other, and giggled.
Then Megan saw Verity lean close to Rubinda, say
something, and then they both laughed.

They're laughing about me, thought Megan. She looked
down at plump Rosie waddling along. *And they're
laughing about Rosie because she's old and smelly.*

Megan began to run, dragging Rosie behind her.
*They'll always be laughing at me if we keep Rosie.
Rosie has got to go,* thought Megan.

Chapter 5

Mum didn't agree that they should get rid of Rosie, but she did take over feeding and walking the dog so that Megan didn't have to. In the house, Megan just pretended that Rosie wasn't there, even when Rosie put her head on Megan's lap under the table at breakfast. *Those girls are going to talk about me and laugh at me again in school,* she thought.

"I don't feel well," said Megan. Mum looked at her and put a hand on her forehead.

"I think you'll be fine, sweetheart. Get your coat on. The walk to school will help."

Mum brought Rosie for the walk. When they got near the school gate, Megan said, "You take Rosie away while I go in."

Megan could see Verity and Rubinda in
the playground. As she went through the school gate,
they saw her and came running over. Megan crossed
her arms and tried to look fierce.

"Hi, Megan!" said Rubinda.

"We want to ask you something," said Verity.

"What?" said Megan, arms still crossed. That "what"
came out a bit like a yappy bark.

"It's about your dog," began Rubinda.

Oh no, thought Megan. "It's not even properly my
dog," she said, in a fierce voice.

Verity took a little step back, but Rubinda reached over
to hold Verity's hand. Rubinda wasn't as easily put off
as Verity was.

"What's the dog called?" said Rubinda. "You see, we saw you in the park and –"

"Laughed," scowled Megan. There was silence for a moment.

Then Rubinda laughed again. "Yes, we did laugh!" she said. "We were guessing your dog's name. I thought it might be Eric, and Verity thought that was funny. Then Verity said it might be Doggy-Doggy-Snuffle-Wuffle." They were both laughing again now, and Megan felt her own mouth twitch. *Are they just being friendly?* she wondered.

"She's called Rosie," said Megan.

"Oh, that's nice!" said Verity. "Better than Doggy-Doggy-Snuffle-Wuffle!"

"She's an old dog," said Megan, watching their faces carefully. Would they laugh? "Sometimes she's a bit smelly."

"So's my cat!" said Rubinda. "I love her so much."

"Is your cat called Catty-Catty-Meow-Lick-Lick?" said Megan.

All three of them were laughing as they sat down at their table in the classroom. It turned out there was plenty of room on it for three.

Chapter 6

Mum came with Rosie to fetch Megan at the end of
the school day. Verity and Rubinda were eager to bend
down and make a fuss of Rosie. And then Rubinda's
mum was talking to Megan's mum, and Verity's dad
came over. Other children came over to pet Rosie too.
She wagged and wagged that stubby little tail and
didn't yap at any of them.

Mum was busy talking, so Megan took Rosie's lead from her, and she let the other children take turns at holding it. They ran around the playground with Rosie waddle-galloping after them, her tongue hanging out.

"She's smiling!" laughed Verity. It did look like that.

"All stand together with Rosie," said Megan's mum. "I'm going to take a photo to send to Mr Toby who used to own Rosie. He'll be so pleased to see her happy."

"Can I send that picture to Lola too?" asked Megan.

When Mum, Rosie and Megan got home, Megan rang Lola. "Did your mum get the photo from my mum?" she asked.

"Yes," said Lola. "That dog with you looks just like the one Mr Toby has."

"It is Mr Toby's dog," said Megan. "He gave me Rosie. I love her."

"Oh, lucky you!" said Lola. "Can I come over and play with her?"

"I'd like that!" said Megan.

But it was Verity and Rubinda who came to Megan's new home first. Mum made her chocolate muffins, which they loved. And this time Megan was hungry for them and ate three, one after another!

Then they went to the park and played ball with Rosie.

A letter for Mr Toby

Dear Mr Toby,

I hope that you are well and happy?

Moving was difficult at first, but I am happy now that I have new friends as well as old ones. Rosie helped me make those new friends. Can you see them all in the photo?

Rosie misses you, but she likes walks and games and hugs with us. We love her.

Do you have new friends in your new place? I hope so. You can show the the photo of Rosie.

Love from Megan

Mr Jim Toby
Bay Tree Care Home

Ideas for reading
Written by Clare Dowdall, PhD
Lecturer and Primary Literacy Consultant

Reading objectives:
- discuss the sequence of events in books and how items of information are related
- draw on what they already know or on background information and vocabulary provided by the teacher
- make inferences on the basis of what is being said and done
- answer and ask questions

Spoken language objectives:
- participate in discussions, presentations, performances and debates
- consider and evaluate different viewpoints, attending to and building on the contributions of others

Curriculum links: PSHE – health and well-being; Writing – composition

Word count: 2505

Interest words: protested, replaced, whimpering, welling, snuffled, waddling

Resources: pencils and papers; materials for making posters: pens, large paper, paints

Build a context for reading

- Ask children about any experiences they have of moving house or school. Create a list of feelings words to describe these experiences on a whiteboard.

- Read the title and blurb. Ask children whether they agree with Megan: that having a puppy would help them to make new friends. Challenge children to think of the advantages and disadvantages of having a new puppy when you move house and start a new school.

- Read the title again: *Oh No, Rosie!*. Ask children what can be inferred about the story from the title (for example, *that Rosie does something wrong*).